The Last Charabanc

J. C. Jones

Copyright © 2024 J. C. Jones

All rights reserved.

ISBN:

DEDICATION

For Ben and Sarah.

Happy 1st Wedding Anniversary.

Cover by Max Jones

A.K.A. Mr. Amillian

CONTENTS

1   THE BOOK

1 THE BOOK

Piere checked the coach one last time. His beautiful black coach glistened in the moonlight. Every part of it had been polished to perfection so that it appeared to shimmer. He walked around it slowly leaving nothing to chance. The lights all worked, there were 4 wheels and they all had tyres. The last thing he needed on the night trip was to be pulled over for a simple traffic infringement.

It was a bitterly cold night and he could see his breath hanging in the air. As he looked around he could see the frost was starting to form on the warehouse windows. It was going to be a deep frost by morning but at least by then the coach would be fully warmed up for its' journey home.

He'd done this run several thousand times before and would likely do it several thousand times more. Still he was a perfectionist and left absolutely nothing to chance. Once he was fully satisfied that the coach was ready, he went back into the office and picked up the passenger manifesto. He cast his eye over the list. Scanning all the names, where they were being picked up from and the time slots he had to arrive at. Originally there had been 1 less passenger on this trip so someone must have booked at the last minute. It didn't really make much difference he had plenty of seats. He made sure his watch was synchronized with the depots clock and went and fired up the coach.

He sprayed the front window with De-Icer once more and flicked the wipers on. Although he had a heated windscreen he had never had much patience. The light frost that had formed didn't take long to clear. He watched it get cleared to the windscreens sides and then slowly slide down the edge.

He was ready, the coach was ready and so he headed back and shut the giant warehouse doors. He locked the doors and put the padlock on. For all the state of the art buses they had the warehouse was straight out of the 1950s. It was just a giant hangar, big enough to get the coaches in and work on. The only heater was in the office and you had almost sit on it to feel any of its' heat. Still it was what it was. It was practical and as the Boss said regularly no customers ever saw the depot.

He jumped back onto the coach and entered all the destinations into the Sat Nav as he let the engine warm up. He felt his heated seat start to warm him up and with that he was ready to start his journey. He stashed the manifesto in his door box, put his seat belt on, put the coach into drive and released the handbrake. His first pick up was only a few miles away and it wasn't going to take long to get there. The roads were very quiet, and the clear night sky made it a good night for driving. Piere always hated it when the rain was lashing down, it always made everything feel so depressing and on top of that the coach didn't handle very well when the roads were awash. He also disliked driving in the fog when many road users didn't know what settings to have their lights on and would invariably either totally blind him or just suddenly appear as if illuminated by just a candle.

The first stop appeared over the horizon and waiting there was an older gentleman. Piere pulled in slowly so as not to firstly startle the passenger, in case they were daydreaming at this hour and hadn't noticed him arriving, and secondly so not to unnerve them with poor driving, nervous passengers could unsettle a whole coach full very quickly. He pressed the button and opened the door. The elderly gentleman just stood at the bottom of the steps looking up at him.

Piere picked up his passenger manifesto from the door.

"Come on board Mr. Walter Briggs."

"Good evening," Walter said as he climbed on board. Piere noted he was very spritely for a man of 75 years of age. He was smartly dressed in a jacket and with a dark woolen over coat finished off with a fine Burgundy scarf around his neck. Piere noted that his brown leather shoes were shined to sheen.

"How are you this evening Walter? You are looking very dapper."

"I'm fine and thank you for saying. One does try to make an effort every now and then."

"Right Walter. I am Piere Darl and I am both your driver and your concierge for your trip. Any questions feel free to ask. I will do my best to answer."

Walter nodded to confirm that he had fully understood what Piere had told him.

"So, you are in seat A1, a window seat. Not much use at night I'm afraid. Do you have any questions?"

Walter laughed, "No, I'm ok thank you Piere. I'm just going to enjoy the ride," and with that he went and found his seat. Piere watched as he got himself settled and then closed the doors. After checking the road in his mirrors for any other vehicles Piere slowly accelerated the coach down the road. Piere looked round a few times to check on Walter as he drove along, but he seemed content just staring out of the window looking at the stars and the moon lit fields.

 The smoothness of the coach meant that the miles disappeared in the rear mirror very quickly. Soon the next pick up was fast approaching and Piere kept his eyes peeled as sometimes people got bored waiting and wondered about a bit. He'd had a few instances where he'd actually had to start hollering people's names out until they eventually appeared. This inevitably always put him behind schedule and in a foul mood. He sighted the next coach stop which was well lit and nicely sheltered. He slowed the coach gently into the stop. Luckily these two had waited where they were supposed to.

Piere pressed the button and opened the door and before him stood Mr. and Mrs. Thomas. A married couple in their early thirties. Very smartly dressed and clearly taking this trip very seriously. They could well have been taking the trip for business reasons for all he knew.

"You must be the Thomas's, good evening to you both. Please come aboard. I am Piere Darl, and I am your driver and concierge this evening. Any questions please feel free to ask."

Mrs. Thomas looked over her shoulder, back at Mr. Thomas. Mr. Thomas motioned his wife forward so he could see Piere clearly. Having moved up a few steps to be in a dominating physical position of the situation Mr. Thomas relaxed. *Obviously an Alpha male* thought Piere.

"Thank you for picking us up promptly, it is appreciated. Will our car be sent to the garage or to our home?"

"Firstly not a problem picking you up, it is all part of the service Mr. Thomas. Secondly, normally the police will send it to a garage. They have to make sure the vehicle is safe before it is allowed back on to the roads. Was there anything else?"

"No, I think that's it."

"Wonderful. Have you two been married long?"

"It's our anniversary tomorrow Piere, we've been married 10 years. That is why we went for a meal this evening with some friends. A little celebration."

"Yes I can see you've both had a drink or two. What is ten years? Is it Tin?"

"Yes Piere but only a few glasses of champagne. And yes ten years is Tin."

"That is lovely. So many couples divorce or split up after a year or two. They don't seem to hang in there with any real commitment to one another."

Mrs. Thomas looked positively smug at these comments and Piere could see she squeezed her husbands' hand tightly in acknowledgement of them as he replied to Piere.

"Oh no, we met at university and have been inseparable ever since. A disastrous first date but several hundred wonderful ones afterwards."

"In this day and age that is so refreshing to hear, congratulations to you both. You should both be very proud. Now you've both had an interesting evening, so take a seat in A3 and A4 for me and kick back and relax. We will soon get you back home."

"Thank you Piere."

Mr. Thomas smiled at Piere and followed his wife to their seats. Piere watched in the rear view mirror to check they were seated before accelerating from the stop. The last thing he wanted was someone rolly pollying down the centre aisle and leaving him a bad review on trip advisor. Piere always tried to be as courteous as he could. He hated being on coaches that were jerky and wanted his passengers to feel more that they were on a train. Nice and smooth, no sudden movements or rapid accelerations or erratic braking. Just relaxing and comfortable. He wanted them to trust him as a driver and have faith in his driving abilities.

The coach rumbled on through the night. Occasionally coming across a random fog patch but nothing to deter Piere from his route. Sometimes the stops were close together but occasionally there could be a bit of drive to the next one. Piere kept his mind on the job knowing that he just had to pick all the passengers up safely and get them to their destination. The next stop soon approached, and he knew there were supposed to be 4 passengers alighting.

The streetlights appeared out of the gloom. This indicated that were now getting into more densely populated areas where the lighting and conditions would be much better. As the Sat Nav notified him that was close to the stop he started decelerating. As the coach slowed he could see that waiting for the coach were 4 late teens, maybe early twenties if they were blessed with very youthful looks. He definitely had not been expecting any passengers to be so young. *Why on earth were they out so late at that age?* He thought to himself.

He pulled the coach up perfectly adjacent to the stop and pressed the button to open the door. He picked up his manifesto from his door to see who was supposed to be boarding. He undid his seatbelt and stepped away from his seat to the stairs that led onto the bus.

"Good evening everyone," Piere said to break the ice, "My name is Piere and I'm your driver and concierge this evening."

There were a few mumblings of hello and alright, so Piere decided to just invite them on and hopefully he had the right 4. The problem with teens is they often used fake IDs so that they could get served beer or cigarettes, thus he had to check each one was the right person getting on.

"Paige Hammond, welcome aboard. Do you have any ID on you?"

Paige stepped forward very confidently for such a young person. *Good upbringing* Piere told himself. Paige stood there looking like a typical metal fan with purple hair and multiple piercings. She had a kind face though, a very reassuring smile.

Paige reached into her bag and produced a Driving License. Piere couldn't see it clearly so had to reach into his jacket and get his glasses out. One of the signs that time was also catching up wih him now. His arms were no longer long enough to read peoples' ID. He scanned her driving license. Checking her name and picture. He looked at her over the top of his glasses.

"You've changed your hair colour a tiny bit, but it's definitely you. Thank you. Seat B1 please."

She shrugged her shoulders and snatched her driving license back. After a few seconds of fumbling she returned it to the compartment in her purse where it lived. With that she disappeared to her seat. Piere had dealt with teens before, they could be angsty with him for no reason and the best course of action was to just carry on. Keep being pleasant and professional. He tried that with his own daughter but she still ignored him most of the time. Speaking to him, or texting him, only when she needed cash. Piere returned to the task in hand.

"Right next I need Miss. Alice Sadler please."

Alice stepped forward and she too was a Goth girl through and through. From the Morticia Addams dress to the white make up and black lipstick and the giant Nu Rock boots that must raise her height by at least 3 inches. It still only made her about 5 foot 4 but it seemed to give her added confidence.

"Good evening, Alice, do you have ID on you please?"

"Certainly but I prefer to be called Saffron."

"I shall make a note of that on my manifesto."

Piere took out the manifesto and next to her name wrote the word Saffron. This simple action made her smile.

Alice handed Piere her Driving License and she was as Gothic looking on that as she was in person.

"Are you a Goth buddy?"

This question took Piere back a little bit. No one had ever asked about his musical tastes before as he drove a coach.

"No Miss, I'm not, I prefer heavy metal. Iron Maiden, Judas Priest, Sabbath. Why do you ask?"

"You're just so pale. You're as white as snow. I need make up to achieve that look."

"Ahh that's working nights for you young lady, driving the coaches and not seeing the sun much except in pictures. Don't think it's affected by my musical preferences."

"It's a good look. And I like a bit of Maiden too."

"Thank you. Alice, I might put some on the CD player in a bit if no one objected. Now you are in seat B2 please."

Piere handed Alice her driving license back and watched her step up into the aisle. Momentarily losing his train of thought thinking about which album to put on, so many good ones to choose from. Shaking his head to get it back in the game when he realised that he was daydreaming.

"Next, I need Mr. Jarrod Jones. Step forward please Sir."

Jarrod stepped forward. He was younger than the others. He looked more nervous too. He obviously knew he shouldn't have been out this late and his dress was more conservative with jeans and a jumper, with a puffer jacket to keep him warm. He was not at this point a fully-fledged goth rocker in fact Piere thought he still had to be at school, or maybe a very young kid at sixth form college.

"Good evening, Jarrod. I assume you don't have ID because of your age?"

"No sir I have my college ID but James here is my brother, he can vouch for me."

"OK Jarrod let's see that college ID."

Jarrod handed him the ID. It was a pretty standard and pretty basic college affair. It was obviously him in the picture and Piere surmised that he must use it to get on campus or access the library or the toilets. It would do for tonight.

"What brings you out so late Jarrod and needing the night coach? You know it's a school night right?"

"James dragged me to some gig. It was alright but very rowdy. I have a revision period first thing so it'll be ok."

"That explains why you're out but I must ask what leaves you needing the night coach?"

"Oh there was a crowd surge, not enough security and we were told we could get a lift home from here. Apparently it was easier all round rather than waiting for a taxi or calling our parents."

"These unlicensed gigs are a nightmare. Always go to reputable concerts Jarrod. Proper security, proper first aid and most importantly much better PA systems."

"I will Sir. Thank you for your advice."

"Good lad, now you're seated in B4."

Piere looked at the remaining member of the group suspecting that it was his idea to come to an abandoned industrial unit for a gig. Risking his younger brother in such a way was against everything that Piere believed in, but he also knew it wasn't his place to judge and young people always pushed the boundaries. Older brothers always dragged younger brothers into deep waters. He laughed at the memories of his older brothers' and their fishing trips. He smiled, composed himself and turned to face James.

"So you must be James."

"You are right."

James stepped forward and thrust his passport into Piere's hand. It was definitely him except in his passport he had much shorter hair and much less denim.

"Well James you are in seat B3."

"Cheers my man."

James shook Piere's hand and walked on to the coach and through to his seat.

Piere was grateful that a lot of the pick ups in the sticks had now been accomplished. They were now heading deeper into the city and the next stop was for multiple people. The majority of the passengers who were on this trip were about to embark. He checked the rear view mirror and made sure that everyone was seated before checking his side mirrors for traffic and heading on. He pressed a button by his dashboard that reminded passengers to buckle up. The alarm kept beeping so someone had not followed the instructions.

He took the coach intercom and began to speak to everyone on board.

"Good evening everyone, can I please ask that you all buckle up your seatbelts. Once you have all done so that annoying beeping noise will stop."

This message clearly got through to everyone as within 30 seconds the beeping had stopped. Piere knew that the lap belts were annoying and even seemed a bit babyish but he couldn't understand people taking the risk of not wearing one. Even if they just improved safety 20% that was definitely worth buckling for. Especially with how some of the idiots drove on the roads these days. Safety was very important for Piere.

There were two problems with driving a coach this size into

the city. First was the number of traffic lights. Surely the authorities could turn them off at this hour. Piere spent most of his time gliding from one traffic light to the next and not seeing a soul as he waited at each red light. He wondered at one stop if he had enough time to get off, get a McDonald's and get back before the lights changed. However there was a very strict no eating and drinking policy on these coaches, so he eventually thought better of it. He actually didn't like McDonald's he just liked the idea of being a rebel for 5 minutes.

The second problem was people just abandoning their cars on the roads. Not parking them as that requires a little bit of forethought and planning. What a lot of people appeared to do was just stop. Stop their car, get out and walk off. Calling it parked. They didn't mind if they parked directly opposite another car as long as they were near their house. However to cap it off was the amount of these drivers who had driveways but didn't use them. Getting the coach through was a nightmare. Piere had spoken to guys and girls in the Emergency services and they too encountered the same problems day in, day out. It was a nightmare.

Still he weaved the coach through the suburban enclaves. Concentrating as hard as he could not to knock a wing mirror or a set of bull bars. He honestly didn't care about their cars but his coach meant the world to him. He was so pleased when it had been wrapped and looked amazing. It was the envy of the rest of the fleet. Sure the rest would be done in time but for now his coach was the standout, the flagship of the fleet. To scratch it would break Piere's heart, not to mention his Boss would probably kick his ass and make him drive one of the old tin cans forever more.

He cautiously made his way to the next stop and pulled in. 22 people were embarking here. This would take strong leadership to get it done efficiently and remain on schedule. He picked up his passenger manifesto, unbuckled his belt and got out of his seat. He had made the choice that he would get them in order before they embarked. He hit the button to open the door and took a deep breath. It was at times like this that he realised not being a people person made his job a little harder.

Stepping down four steps of the coach's entrance he was now on the bottom step of the coach, and he had primed himself to be the Alpha dog of this situation, or at least convince the passengers that he was. He stood there clipboard in hand and surveyed the sea of faces that was staring back at him. Every time he had to do this he felt nervous. He thought after so many trips he might find it a little easier, but he never did. He still felt his mouth go as dry as the Sahara Desert, his leg developed go – go gadget syndrome and shook uncontrollably, and he felt everyone looking at him was taking the piss out of him. Still once again he tried.

"Ladies and Gentlemen good evening. My name is Piere Darl and tonight I am your driver and your concierge. If you need anything just ask. I am going to call your names out. Please make yourself known to me when I do so by stepping forward. Firstly can I have Mrs. Leanne Forrester please."

The crowd murmured and shuffled about. All looking about to see who Leanne was. Piere saw a lady heading his way. He looked down at the lady who had pushed her way to the front. She was tiny. She wasn't 5 foot tall with her beret on. Her face was etched with a lifetime of memories, but for all her age she stood bolt upright and fixed his gaze without a hint of intrepidation.

"Mrs. Leanne Forrester?" Piere enquired of her.

She shuffled her walking stick so she could lean on it using both hands in front of her.

"I am indeed Sir. Do you know I've been stood here waiting for you for nearly two hours?"

"No Mrs. Forrester I was unaware of that."

"I am 94 years of age; I should not have been left standing that long. Would you have left your mother there that long?"

"I can not agree more, so to take you off those sore feet how about you take a seat for me in seat A2 next to Walter."

"Is that far?"

"No, that is the nearest seat I have available."

"Good, the nurses in my home said you would be quick!"

"Madame, I have been as quick as I possibly could have been. To the point where I have even called your name out first from my list. That is how important you are to me."

"Well I should think so."

"Do you need a hand onto the coach?"

"I am old, I am not an invalid."

"Point taken Mrs. Forrester. If you need anything else I can do, please let me know!"

"Don't you worry Mr. Darl, I got you on speed dial!"

With that Leanne hustled her way onto the Coach and took her seat next to Walter Briggs. For someone who was claiming that they were infirm she moved like a Sherman Tank. Piere decided to let it ride and deal with it if she came back to him. *Christ some old people were scary* he thought to himself. She would have also been aware what the pickup time was. He was on time, the fact she got there early was not his fault although she clearly blamed him for not being early. He wasn't going to point this out though. Sometimes an argument was lost before it began and it was like trying to play chess with a pigeon, sooner or later they would knock all the pieces over and shit on the board.

Piere ran his hand over his shaven head, trying to wipe away any sweat that was showing his discomfort. It was not a great start to being the Alpha dog, he just hoped that the rest of the passengers were not as cantankerous as Mrs. Forrester. If they were, in theory he could refuse them entry. All he wanted was a simple life, after all he was just doing a job.

"Right Ladies and Gentlemen can I get the Potter family please to the front please."

Piere watched as Mr. Potter led his family through the throng. He was the size of a mountain bear. Piere wondered if one seat would be enough for him. He must have 6 foot 10 inches tall and weighed 25 stone. Piere couldn't remember ever seeing a man so large in his whole life. He stood on the kerb as Piere was on the coach and he was still taller than him. His wife following in his wake was barely 5 foot two and looked as delicate as an English Rose. Piere had many questions but decided against all of them in case Mr. Potter snapped him in half just using one hand. It was however proof that opposites attract. The two children were just doing as they were told. They were very well behaved children, which Piere liked. Unruly children could, and had in the past, caused him to have very uncomfortable journeys. All the other passengers end up getting ratty with one another and thus, in turn, they got ratty with him.

"Good evening Mr. Potter, thank you for your patience. I assume this is Helen, Mark and Finn."

"You are correct. Where's our luggage?"

"Mr. Potter all personal items are dealt with by our sister company. They go freight. Everything you need will be sent to your destination."

"That's good because those Nintendo Wii's are not cheap to buy and if you lose them I'll be suing your ass."

"That's fair enough Mr. Potter, but please judge us on what we achieve not we hypothetically might not."

Piere felt his confidence growing a bit with every conversation he was having. He had expected Mr. Potter's voice to be a booming noise but instead it was very calm and collected. Obviously a man who saw no need in asserting himself any further than his enormous frame already did.

"Hi I'm Finn."

The elder of the two children spoke up and introduced himself. Piere was impressed how polite the boy was.

"Good evening, Finn, I'm Piere. How has your day been?"

"My day was good thank you. We went shopping, I helped dad plumb in a new gas cooker and now I get to go on a road trip."

"Well Finn that sounds like a fantastic day, you might even have a snooze on your journey to replenish your batteries."

"I'm just fine thank you."

"Well, Finn, the option is there. Mr. Potter, your seats are C1, C2, C3 and C4. Please make yourself comfortable and remember any questions please fire away."

"Thank you Piere, I'll get the kids settled and be up for a chat, maybe just a break you know what I mean?!" Mr. Potter said and followed it up with booming laugh that filled the night air.

"Yes Mr. Potter I do indeed. Feel free to come and chat with me any time you want a little respite."

Piere understood a little bit about parenting even though his own daughter would have claimed he didn't know a thing, especially about her. Sometimes it was just about being able to offer an option. Kids often got restless on journeys, and he was well versed in showing children the layout of his cab and letting them pull the air horn was often a go to measure for ensuring peace, for 5 minutes anyway!

He watched the Potter family take their seats and get settled. He hated it when people got on to quickly and everyone got in everyone else's way. It was way easier to let one group get on, get comfy and then send the next group through. It not only saved time in the long run, but it often stopped confrontation. Travel was stressful and he saw a key part of his job to be keeping stress to a minimum. It worked in his favour too, if the passengers were less stressed it made his journeys less stressful. Driving a big coach wasn't easy and took a lot of concentration and if his passengers were bickering and arguing then that distracted him and thus put all his passengers on edge. It was a kind of mad version of ever decreasing circles where all faults would eventually lie at his cab door.

Piere breathed deeply through his nose and took a look at his roster. He was trying to figure out the quickest and easiest way of getting the next 17 people on board. As he scanned the roster he decided who was next.

"Mrs. Mumford? Where are you?"

A young lady came forward carrying a baby who was swaddled up in a blanket. Piere smiled when he saw her. The baby looked lovely and warm, with a little blue hat on his head to keep him warm.

"Shall we get you and you baby in the warm sweetheart?"

"I'd like that."

"Have you been crying?"

Piere couldn't help but notice her eyes were sunken and red raw. She looked as if she had been crying for days. She also had a slightly disheveled look, a look many new parents have until they get into a proper routine where the baby lets them sleep for at least a few unbroken hours. He himself as a parent had got quite used to wondering around with clothes on that had various deposits on from his daughter.

"I'm ok now. David has stopped crying now and has finally gone to sleep. I'm sure he'll wake up to be fed in a bit though."

"Ok Mrs. Mumford, I'll take your word for it. Enjoy the peace before he wakes up. Just remember you're safe now. Any problems you come and see me, ok?"

"I will. Thank you Piere."

"I'll put you in D1 and D2, make yourself at home. Relax and enjoy the ride."

A thin smile crept across Mrs. Mumford's' mouth as she boarded holding her child who could not have been more than 6 months old. Piere didn't mind babies on the coach as long as they didn't scream the place down. In fact a sleeping baby was perfect and with a little luck the rhythm of the coach rolling along would assist in keeping the baby asleep for the whole journey. Who knows, perhaps Mrs. Mumford might even be able to grab half an hour's snooze herself, she looked as if she needed it.

Piere checked his watch. He was a little behind schedule but as soon as he got the rest of these on board, he'd be back on time… if they settled quickly. *Ah well fingers crossed* he thought to himself.

Next on the list were the Pearce's.

"Jeff and Andrew Pearce, where are you?"

Piere scanned the people and saw two Lycra clad cyclists were heading his way along with a tandem bike with a buckled front wheel.

"I can see why you two need a lift! That wheel's seen better days."

"Yeah, hit a parked car didn't we. We were told we could put the bike in the luggage bay. Is that ok?"

"Not a problem lads. Follow me," Piere said before turning back to the rest who were gathered, "No one get on until I get back, am I clear?"

There were a few murmurings from the gathered rabble, but Piere thought he had said it sternly enough that they got the gist of it. He made his way to the coach's side and undid the luggage flap.

"There you go lads, slide it in there."

The Pearce's carefully put their bike on its' side and positioned it so that they were happy it wouldn't slide about too much. It looked like a very expensive bike, not that Piere was an expert.

"You haven't got helmets lads? All the gear from the shirts to the shorts to the clip on shoes, but no helmets?"

"We like to feel the breeze running through our hair, it's exhilarating," Jeff said very excitedly.

"We feel freedom without helmets, although when we're racing we have to wear them, which is a drag," Andrew piped in.

"Yeah the races have so many rules," Jeff dejectedly added.

Piere just shrugged his shoulders and shut the luggage compartment up making sure he locked it so no one would steal the bike.

"Right lads on you get, you're in seats," Piere paused to double check his manifesto, "D3 and D4, no fighting over the window seat."

The two cyclists clip clopped their way on to the coach with their specialist cycling shoes. Piere was glad it wasn't raining tonight otherwise those two would've been slip sliding down all the way down the aisle and more than likely gone arse over tit, and that definitely would've got him a bad review. Piere couldn't help but feel that social media was taking over so much but only in negative ways. People only ever use it to criticize or point out minor failings. No one ever said how clean the bus was, or how personable he was, or how the toilet was so fresh.

Returning to his step on the coach he once again picked up his manifesto. Scanning down the names he picked one out.

"Next I need Rachel Freeman, where are you Rachel?"

Rachel made her presence known and walked to the front. She was a lady in her mid-50s and she was immaculately dressed. She could've been going to a wedding. Beautiful navy blue pin striped trouser suit with matching clutch handbag. Piere was staggered by her beauty and elegance to the point of nearly being tongue tied.

"Ahh good evening Rachel. How are you today?"

"I'm feeling wonderful. I was starting to think that I'd never get out of that hospital."

"Well you are out, and you are free. Can you please take up seat E1 please."

"I'd love to, it'll be lovely just to see something other than hospital walls."

And just like that she bounded onto the coach. *At least this evening's commuters were varied* Piere thought. Sometimes he had the joy of 50 football fans to transport and they were always a pain. Singing and chanting. Tonight's ensemble were very pleasant so far. The adults were behaving and all the children were well mannered.

He ticked off the names that had successfully got on the coach and chose the next passengers to be allowed on.

"Next I need Derek and Margaret Grimes please."

The Grimes came forward, they looked very solemn, the complete opposite of Rachel and this brought Piere back down to the ground with a real bump.

"Mr. and Mrs. Grimes you don't look very happy. Can I help?"

"No sir, we're just a little sad. It's been a dreadful day what with our home and possessions having all been burnt to the ground. But we were told to come here and that something would be sorted for us."

"I'm very sorry to hear that. Must be a great upheaval for you. However you are correct we can help, so do not worry, you are safe now."

"Thank you Sir."

"Not a problem, and please call me Piere. Could you take up seats E3 and E4 for me please."

"Shall do Piere."

Piere thought he detected a hint of smile in Mrs. Grimes, as well as a distinct smell of smoke emanating from their clothes and hair. His mind drifted as he watched them. It can be devastating to lose everything but at least they still had each other, some people don't even have that. And possessions are just things. Items can be replaced and homes can be rebuilt. Some people just didn't see the big picture initially, but they always do in time. Hopefully everything was insured and the insurers don't try playing hard ball.

"Right moving on have I got Michelle Ovette?"

"Good evening, Michelle, can I ask you to put that cigarette out for me before boarding please?"

"Of course you can sweetie."

Michelle was dressed more for a night out on the town than a coach trip, but Piere reasoned that everyone was different. She was quite clearly quite a fan of partying and Piere wondered if he should search her bag to make sure she wasn't trying to smuggle alcohol on board. He stopped that thought immediately as he realised he was inadvertently profiling her which he knew was very much frowned upon.

Piere watched as Michelle stubbed her cigarette out under her stiletto and very gracefully alighted the steps onto the coach.

"How are you this evening Michelle?"

"I'm ok, bit confused I suppose as to why I'm here."

"Oh, how so Michelle?"

"Well I was partying with my friends. Few drinks and then I was told to wait here for my ride home."

"Drink and drugs can cause confusion Michelle, they do alter the minds perception of time and space, it is very late and perhaps your good Samaritan friends just wanted to make sure you were safe.

Michelle nodded and gave a very cheeky smile.

"Now Michelle could you take up seat E2 for me please, and if you need anything please just ask."

"Is there a bathroom on board?"

"Yes Michelle it's at the back on the left and don't forget to lock the door."

"Thank you sweetie."

Michelle breezed past him and gave him a kiss on the cheek which caused Piere to instantly blush. He was generally very staid and any form of human contact made him feel slightly anxious. Still he knew she had meant well and that it was just a friendly gesture.

Piere looked at his manifesto as he used his sleeve to wipe his cheek clean of any lipstick. Having lipstick on his face was a very unprofessional look. The next eight were all an army transfer. He looked at the crowd and counted eight men in army uniforms. You could always spot them even without uniform. They all walked in time, a kind of march that they couldn't shake off even when being civilians.

"Gentlemen welcome aboard. When I call your name could you step forward and proceed to the seat I assign please."

"YES SIR!" In unison all eight replied, a lot louder than Piere had imagined they would. He was at least now fully awake, as were half the neighbours in the vicinity of the coach.

"Samuel Ellis," Piere called out, "F1"

"Where shall I put my kit bag Sir?"

Piere realised that they were all carrying kit bags.

"We'll put them in the luggage hold, follow me."

Piere unlocked the other luggage hold.

"Have they all got your names on?" Piere asked not wanting a kerfuffle when they reached their destination with everyone trying to work out who's bag was who's.

"Yes Sir. Name, Rank and Regiment," Samuel replied which was music to Piere's ears.

"Perfect, you can all stash them in here for the duration journey."

The soldiers all stowed their bags away accordingly and Piere locked the compartment up so that they were safe.

"Thank Samuel, and you are seat F1."

"Thomas Kendrick, F2, Peter Smith, F3. Paul Tilley F4."

After Paul got on Piere waited a few seconds and went and checked that they had all found their seats and the aisle on the coach was not a scene of chaos. Once satisfied he went back out and continued his roll call.

"Adrian Hendry please, G1. Marcos Jenkins G2."

As Marcos got on Piere could just see a silhouette hustling down the road towards him quickly. Piere hoped this was the final passenger as he did not want to be waiting around. They were about 200 yards away and making good progress so Piere felt a sense of relief.

"Right where was I. Ah yes Ryan Unsworth G3. And that hopefully leaves you to be Robert Price."

"Yes sir!"

"Well Robert you are in G4."

"Thank you Sir, God am I glad to be back home. It was a hell hole out there."

"I can imagine it was awful but Robert you are now home safe and sound. Please enjoy the ride, G4 don't forget!"

Robert practically skipped onto the coach just as the final passenger arrived before Piere.

"I'll let you catch your breath."

"Thank you, I didn't think I was going to make it and I was told not to miss it or there'd be hell to pay later on."

"It would mess a lot of my schedule up but you are here now and I assume you are Ian Jinks?"

"Yes, that's me."

Ian was hunched over hands on his knees and slowly getting his breathing under control.

"Are you ok Ian?"

"Yes, I'm all good. Just been a very busy day that's all. Solo climbed The Scar peak this morning and then I lost my phone which had my bank cards in it but luckily I was offered a seat on here so I could get home as quickly as possible and hopefully before anyone worries."

"I'm sure everyone is fine and we will have you sorted out as quickly as I can drive the coach."

"Wicked brother!"

"Right Ian you are in seat H1."

With Ian on board and seated Piere did a quick sweep to make sure no one had left anything behind for which he would have to turn the coach round and come back for. He had learnt that this was the easiest way to do it as a three point turn in a coach this size often became an 87 point turn with lots of helpful advice from the passengers. Satisfied that the area was clear he too got on the coach and shut the door.

He stood motionless at the front of the coach and was ready to address the passengers. He noted everyone was sitting down and paying him attention, when they were attentive it made relaying instructions much easier. As he cast his eye over them he was pleased at how all the seats looked so smart. The black leather, well faux leather looked very sharp. It truly was a luxury coach. The seats all reclined, individual air controls and plenty of leg room. *Unless you were Mr. Potter* he guessed. He checked Michelle was back from the toilet and with a quick head count he confirmed all passengers were present and listening.

"Good evening everyone welcome aboard. You can eat and drink, but no alcohol is to be consumed on this coach. I just want to ask that when we arrive you take all your rubbish with you, and bear in mind I know where you've sat!!! The toilet is at the back of the Coach, if the light is on above the door then it is in use, that will hopefully save you a wasted trip. Can I ask you all to buckle up your seatbelts, we are driving at night and there are unexpected dangers out there. We still have a few stragglers to pick up but it won't take us much time. Now sit back and relax. I shall now get this show on the road."

He still hated talking to crowds and he was glad that it was over for now. It definitely wasn't in the job description, driving the coach was, but public speaking was not.

Piere sat down in the drivers' seat, put the manifesto safely back in his door and buckled up his seat belt. He was pleased that when he put the Seat Belt sign on there was no beeping. This meant everyone was buckled in securely. He checked the mirrors and eased the coach back onto the road. Within a few hours this trip would all be over and he'd be on the return leg. He enjoyed driving the coach on his own. No one critiqued his driving and he could put his music on as loud as he wanted.

The coach had travelled maybe three or four miles before the first seat belt was unbuckled. He checked the rear view mirror and saw the young Finn Potter heading up the aisle to the toilet. What he hadn't noticed was Mrs. Thomas had also unbuckled her seat belt at the exact same moment and was making her way past her husband towards him. Thus he was slightly shocked when she just appeared beside him. *Didn't anyone ever pay attention to the sign that said do not distract the driver?* He thought to himself.

"Piere?" she quietly uttered.

"Yes Mrs. Thomas."

"I was just talking with my husband and we don't recognise some of these roads. Are we going in the right direction?"

"Mrs. Thomas, sometimes I can't get the coach down the quickest routes so the ones that you might use in your car are not available to me. I can assure you that everything is in hand. Also Mrs. Thomas at night things look so different. The light catches some things and not others. So you don't need to worry."

"That's good Piere, will it be much longer until we arrive?"

"Not at all, I have a few pick ups that will delay us slightly but soon enough we will arrive at your destination."

"Thank you Piere."

She tapped him on the shoulder and made her way back to her seat seemingly reassured. A few seconds later the beeping stopped so Finn must have also returned to his seat from the toilet. Piere relaxed and kept his eyes on the road. He had seen on the Sat Nav that the next pick up was pretty soon so he hoped that there wouldn't be any more interruptions before that.

It was a new stop for him, in all his years he hadn't ever stopped the coach there. Piere disliked being on unfamiliar ground. He was stuck in his ways like that, he didn't like change all that much. If it had been up to him he'd have made them get on at one of the regular stops. However his boss had pointed out they were valued customers and the nearest stop to them was miles away. Piere had bitten his tongue and knew when he was beaten. At the end of the day he was paid to drive and pick up the passengers, and his Boss was paid to keep passenger numbers up and keep the shareholders happy.

As he slowed the coach down he could see it was an old brick style bus stop. He hadn't seen one of these in years. He thought they had been demolished a long time ago to stop vagrants living in them.

Obviously they'd missed one. His coach was clearly going to be far too big for the actual stop as well, this was getting better by the second. He'd make a note of it on his manifesto and with any luck he would never, ever, have to stop here again.

He was only picking up 2 passengers so with any luck it wouldn't take too long. Breeze them on, get them sorted and be on his way as quickly as possible.

With the coach stopped he put on the hazard lights. It was night time so anyone driving about would, in theory, see his lights and not rear end his pristine coach. He'd had it happen a few years back when some lady putting on her make up on didn't spot he'd stopped at a traffic light. So much paperwork and faff. About the only time Piere had ever been grateful for traffic cameras capturing what happened.

Right back to the job in hand he told himself, concentrate. He picked up his manifesto, unbuckled his seat belt, undid the doors and started making his way off the coach. Before he'd even got to the second step he was aware of a passenger hurtling down the aisle towards him.

"Are you ok Michelle?"

"Yep, yep fine Piere. Just wondering if I had time for a quick cigarette?"

Piere looked at her very seriously, she'd only stubbed one out as she embarked and that had to be less than twenty minutes ago.

"No, not this time Michelle. I will be stopping in half an hour for everyone to stretch their legs though. I hope that will ok for you. Please go back to your seat. Sooner I get these passengers aboard the sooner we can get to our planned break."

Michelle looked dreadfully crestfallen, stood there with her cigarette in her mouth ready to light, but Piere knew give one an inch and the whole lot would take two miles and he'd end up behind schedule with his Boss chewing his ear off. He looked out of the coach. There was no one there. He re-checked his schedule, it definitely said there should be two people here. Tentatively he made his way to the bus shelter. As he peered into the gloom he could see a silhouette. As his eyes adjusted he could clearly see that there inside were two young lads fast asleep.

"Ahem."

There was no response, not even a slight stirring.

"Ahem!" That much louder announcement of his presence stirred them both immediately, "sorry for keeping you up so late!"

They both jumped up with a jolt.

"It's ok gentleman. Take it easy. My name is Piere Darl and I am your driver and Concierge this evening."

They were obviously both so tired that they just decided to trust him. He could've been a crazed axe murderer for all they knew.

"Sorry, just a bit tired been a long day," the first one said. He was in his late 30s, unshaven and looked like a hiker. The walking boots, crampons, Norwegian walking sticks.

"And you are?" Piere enquired.

"Michael Newman."

"And you went hiking in this weather?"

"Oh Piere, was it?"

"Yes I am Piere,"

"Good, we hike in all weathers. See the Earth as it is in all its' glories and in all seasons."

"Wonderful. Not my cup of tea to be honest lads but I'm glad you enjoy it. And that means you must be Tyronne Meadows?"

"Yes I am."

"And are also a hiker?"

"We call ourselves ramblers Piere."

"Let's not split hairs Tyronne, you go out walking in fields!" Piere replied with a cheeky grin. .

"Yes, today wasn't the best day for it though," Tyronne continued, "It was windy and cold. The views weren't great."

Piere inhaled and sought eye contact with the young man, "That, Tyronne, is because it hasn't got above 0 degrees centigrade all day and it's blowing a gale. Right let's get you two on the bus and thawed out. Michael you are in seat H3 and Tyronne you are in H4. Shall we stash you ruck sacks in the luggage compartment?"

"That would be wonderful, thank you Piere. Can we put the Nordic Poles in there as well."

"There is plenty of room for all your kit."

Piere opened up the luggage compartment. His main reason for this was he did not want their soaking kit dripping on his luxury interior. The two hikers stowed their gear away. Piere could see that they were both very keen to get on the coach and warm up.

"H3 and H4 guys. And don't forget to buckle up once you are sat down. Remember safety first."

The two field dwellers, as Piere would know them as for the rest of this journey, made their way down the aisle and soon settled. Piere followed his usual routine and soon the coach was back on the road with just one stop left to make and then all the passengers would be collected. One rest break to make and that would be it. Within two hours this whole journey would be completed. Another one ticked off. It was normally around this point that Piere wished he was paid by the mile and not salaried but he knew in the long run salaried was better. Especially when there were quieter months with fewer passengers and less trips to be made. It meant he was at least financially stable. *Perhaps I should ask for a bonus if I do over so many miles a month?* He thought to himself. *Or maybe I could push for a drivers' seat that massages as well as heats!* This was all starting to form as a giant plan in Piere's head. *It might even attract new drivers* he thought to himself.

The coach rumbled along eating up the miles. Piere was back on roads he knew and in cruise control. Looking out for little landmarks he recognised. Certain landmarks meant a certain amount of time until he got to another point. The bright pink house at the end of a set of S bends meant exactly 1 mile until a set of traffic lights that no one ever crossed at but always went red as he approached, the thatched house meant that he was exactly 10 minutes from the next stop, and the broken down tractor just sitting on the verge, that he had been watching rust away for the last 5 years, meant he had less than a minute until his final stop was done.

Piere lost himself in thought about how certain landmarks meant certain things. He remembered being a young child and how he and sister used to competitively look out of the car window to be the first one to be the sea when going on holiday to Torquay. In all relevance it made no difference. However as a child the first to see it was technically the first one on holiday. He cast his mind to the journey home and the first one to see the big boulder before their turning was also the first one to be home. Strategic markers used by the memory. He thought about asking the field dwellers if they did the same sort of thing on their trips but he didn't want to invade their personal space, plus he had a coach to drive and the idea of stopping the journey for a little natter might upset his Boss.

He slowed the coach down and pulled into the next stop, luckily he knew it well and it was a properly sized coach stop designed for modern coaches. He'd get that other one fixed if they were about to start using it regularly. It could be quite dangerous otherwise; someone could get hurt.

He undid himself and picked up his schedule. Mr. and Mrs. Kennedy. Holiday makers heading home. As Piere saw them he could see they were both early 70s and both looking pretty spritely, the way they sprang out of the coach stop seats as soon as he approached.

"Good evening Mr. and Mrs. Kennedy how are you both?"

"Feeling good thank you. Looking forward to getting home," Mrs. Kennedy answered very enthusiastically. *Must be the little blue pill* thought Piere.

"I am Piere, I am your driver and your concierge this evening any thing you need just let me know."

"Can we store our suitcases on the coach?" Mr. Kennedy asked.

"Much easier to put them in the luggage hold sir, perfectly safe and no need for you to worry. Follow me."

Piere jumped off the coach and headed toward the luggage compartment. He decided to put them with the field dwellers' equipment.

"So have you been on holiday Mr. Kennedy?"

"Yes. Yes we have," Mr. Kennedy replied.

"My lungs have been playing up a bit and the doctor advised lots of exercise and fresh air," Mrs. Kennedy interjected.

"Well there are plenty of hills to walk around here and the air is fresh, you chose a perfect destination," Piere replied. He had heard of the therapeutic nature of the moorlands before.

"I couldn't walk too far, or too high but I got far enough didn't I Phillip?" Mrs. Kennedy answered.

"You did the best you could sweetheart, and at least your cough has stopped now," Mr. Kennedy replied.

"That is true Phillip. Very true. Piere I have been plagued by this cough for a year now and I come here, fresh air, exercise on the hills and boom it's gone," Mrs. Kennedy joyfully told Piere.

"That is fantastic news Mrs. Kennedy. Long may it continue.," Piere said as he secured their bags in the hold, "Right let's get you on board. You are in seats 11 and 12. Please buckle up once you are settled."

"Of course we will Piere," Mrs. Kennedy replied.

Mr. Kennedy looked slightly downbeat as he boarded the coach but Piere knew many people did when their holidays ended and they had to go back to grind of their normal lives. It can really take the wind out of your sails. The joy and freedom of a holiday ends and going back to your mundane existence pretending to like your neighbours, care about mowing the grass and do the housework can be an absolute chore. Mr. Kennedy was obviously a lover of being on holiday. Piere fully understood that. He remembered back to his childhood and the internal agony he felt of leaving the beach for the last time to go and pack to go home, to go back to normality and back to school. He could fully emphasize with Mr. Kennedy on this one.

  With everyone seated and settled Piere went through his usual ritual and slowly the coach exited its' last passenger stop. Another car approached from the distance and like many others didn't dip its' headlights until Piere was completely blinded. He wasn't sure if it was driver ignorance or too many people relying on automatic light controls. Either way it made him feel pretty annoyed.

The seatbelt alarm went off and Piere flicked his eyes up to the rear view mirror. He could see both Jeff and Andrew Pearce approaching him. What do they want he thought to himself. The larger brother Andrew stepped down beside Piere's cab, Jeff stood slightly behind him.

"Good evening gentlemen, how can I be of assistance?" Piere asked.

There was a silence and the two brothers looked at one another as Jeff implored his brother to speak.

"Well Piere, Jeff and I have been talking and well… well neither of us could remember booking a coach to pick us up?" Andrew just managed to splutter out.

"You must have booked a ticket gentlemen otherwise I wouldn't have you on my manifesto, I wouldn't have known to pick you up would I?"

The two brothers again looked at one another. They both looked puzzled, Piere's logic was impeccable.

"You boys must have crashed quite hard, and without helmets there is a good chance of a concussion at least," Piere stated pretty matter of factly, "do either of you feel sick or dizzy?"

"I've never felt better," Jeff replied.

"Same here Piere. If the bike hadn't had damage on it I wouldn't have realised we'd been in a crash," Jeff was clearly very confused and trying to remember what had happened.

"Best bet lads, have a seat, have a rest and I'm sure it will all come flooding back to you."

The two brothers were obviously not satisfied but took Piere's advice. Piere watched them return to their seats, they stopped and spoke to several other passengers on their way. Perhaps they know one another Piere rationalised to himself and as soon as the seat belt light went out he turned his complete concentration back to the road ahead.

It was only a few more miles before the seat belt light flashed again. Piere checked his mirror once more. This time it was Mr. Potter heading in his direction. The giant haystack of a man sat on the step next to the cab, Piere glanced to his left and saw they were the same height, except Piere was on a seat.

"Good evening Mr. Potter. What can I do for you?"

"Sorry to bother you Piere but does this coach have wi-fi?"

"Of course it does Mr. Potter. All lower case with no spaces 'road due boy!'

Piere could see the relief on his face at this news and the fact it was accessible."

"Thank you Piere, kids are driving me bonkers."

"They're only young Mr. Potter, we were all young once."

Mr. Potter laughed.

"Do you mind if I sit here for a few minutes Piere? The peace and quiet is lovely."

Piere felt sorry for Mr. Potter. A man who quite simply liked quiet time and tranquility.

"Ok Mr. Potter a few minutes but for safety you will have to go back to your seat then."

Mr. Potter nodded that he both understood and agreed. He then shut his eyes and started breathing very deeply. Piere laughed to himself and carried on watching the road. The road started to twist and turn as the coach began ascending an enormous hill. The safety barriers shone as the coaches' headlights bounced off them at certain angles. Mr. Potter rubbed his face to wake himself up. He put one hand on Piere's door to help steady his gigantic frame as he rose to his feet.

"Piere,"

"Yes Mr. Potter?"

"Where are we going?"

Mr. Potter looked particularly confused. Piere rubbed his forehead and glanced sideways at Mr. Potter.

"Mr. Potter you need to give your children the wi-fi password and have a good sleep. You must be exhausted."

"I am very tired Piere."

"Good go and have a rest and we'll soon be there; you booked the tickets."

Mr. Potter headed back into the coach and the seat belt light went out. Piere concentrated hard as these roads were quite treacherous. Every so often he glanced in the rear view mirror. He could see more and more passengers chatting to one another. It was always interesting to Piere that they could all get on as strangers and then chat away to one another like long lost school buddies. They probably confessed more to strangers than they ever would to people who they were actually friends with. A sort of therapy, he often thought of recording the conversations and releasing them as a book. Even after many years he still found it fascinating so why wouldn't other people. An insight into his life. *One day I will* he told himself, *I will release confessions heard by the coach driver.*

The coach continued climbing and the roads got narrower and the bends tighter, Piere was pleased that the visibility was so good and that it was dry. He'd done this route before when there had been near zero visibility and roads felt like glass. He hadn't enjoyed those trips one bit. Knowing full well that one mistake and he would send the coach careering hundreds of feet to the bottom of the hill. He had even joked with some of his colleagues that even if he survived the fall then his Boss would kill him anyway.

He noticed in the mirror that some of his passengers were now deep in discussion. He prayed they weren't talking politics as that always ended in an argument. He tried to listen in and keep an eye on it but he had to concentrate on the road. The snippets he saw he could tell that some were getting animated, he saw a few clearly gesticulating in his direction. Sometimes the voices were raised, sometimes they whispered. He could feel something brewing behind him. He knew the road would level out soon enough. He kept plowing on, hoping to see a landmark that meant the top was imminent and the roads would improve.

There it was. The burnt out shell of the old Hill Top Hotel came into view. No one had ever fixed it, must have been years since it burnt down. Perhaps there was a delay with the insurance. He thought back to the passengers he used to pick up there after a riotous night of partying or the night of the fire when everyone just wanted to get back to the nearest town. He dismissed it all from his mind as the seat belt light came. He flicked his eyes at the rear view mirror. It was the army lads all heading his way. He knew he had a few hundred yards and the roads would improve dramatically and make his life a lot easier. It was tiring getting this coach round all the hair pin bends.

"Piere," the first soldier announced, "We have a few questions we'd like answered."

"Fire away gentlemen," Piere replied.

"We want to know when we will arrive at our destination,"

"That's a very reasonable request, according to my Sat Nav, we will be there in 45 minutes. That is dependent on traffic and road conditions of course, but it's normally pretty accurate."

"Thank you Piere. My, I mean our, second question is where is our destination?"

"Do you mean ultimately or on this coach?"

The soldier looked befuddled,

"I guess on this coach Piere," the soldier replied.

Piere jammed on the brakes as hard as he could and sent the soldiers who were standing flying. The first one, Ryan Unsworth, banged his head hard on the windscreen.

"What are you playing at Piere?" the disgruntled soldier asked as he picked himself up out of the stair well.

"Did you not see the deer? I'm gonna have to ask you to take your seat. You could've hurt yourself! Deer travel in Rangales, so where there is one there will be ten at least," Pierre said staring out onto the road in front of him.

"Piere?"

"Take your seat now please!" Piere stated very definitely. Leaving the soldier in no doubt to retreat from the cab area.

Piere watched them take their seats once more. They were now chatting even more animatedly. He also noted more and more passengers becoming involved in the discussion. He tried to keep an eye on people but it was impossible to watch them all. He attempted to just concentrate on the road ahead. It wouldn't be long until they could all have a break and stretch their legs. Being couped up on a coach could affect people.

He saw the seat belt light come on. He looked up and saw several of the army lads walking up the coach, kneeling down and talking to the other passengers. He was acutely aware that more and more of the passengers were now unbuckled. Piere squeezed the bridge of his nose, hoping they would all come to their senses soon enough but the longer it went on then the likelihood of that happening diminished greatly.

As he watched what was occurring in his rear view mirror he tried to keep up the pretense he wasn't, he attempted to keep as cool as possible. He could see whatever was being said was having three distinct affects. Some passengers were getting angry, some were in shock and some looked incredibly upset. The volume in the coach was escalating well above what was an acceptable level. The sheer number of passengers no longer wearing their seat belts meant that Piere's hand was being forced. He always tried to be fair with his passengers so they could have an enjoyable trip however this was becoming intolerable. Within a few minutes he was unsure if anyone, except Walter, was still wearing their seat belt. *Did they not understand the importance of safety?* He thought to himself. He took the coach intercom and started talking to the passengers en masse.

"Ladies and Gentlemen could I please ask you all to return to your allocated seats and put your seat belt back. This is a safety precaution."

No one moved, the volume increased and now there were even more passengers stood up.

"Ladies and gentlemen if you do not sit down and put your seat belts on I will be forced to stop the coach immediately until my request is compiled with."

Piere looked at the rear view mirror as again no one did as they were asked. He rubbed his face with his hand, took another look in the mirror but there was no change.

Piere realised that the passengers were now beyond any form of reasonable control. This inevitably happened on every trip eventually. Sometimes sooner, sometimes later. It made no real difference. The calls were getting louder and passengers growing in confidence as often happens with a mass gathering or a mob. He knew that it wouldn't be long before the mob mentality overruled any sense of good judgement amongst the passengers and would put his safety at risk. He decided he had to act now.

Just up ahead Piere knew there was a layby that he could pull into, as he had many times before, and when it appeared, looming out of the gloom, he did so. As smoothly as he had done with every single stop on the journey. He undid his seat belt and turned back into the coach to face the mob. He noticed Walter was still staring out of the window. Almost oblivious to everything going on around him.

"Ladies and gentlemen, please take your seats."

He looked at the gathered crowd and they were not for moving. They all stood firmly facing him still. The army lads front and centre. Taking charge of the growing mutiny.

"I SAID TAKE YOUR SEATS AND DO IT NOW!" His voice boomed over them all, shocking everyone with its' sheer volume and force.

He made it abundantly clear that he was not playing. The first few rows who were directly in front of him did so. He knew when one soldier obeyed the others would quickly follow suit, it was in their training to do so. The army lads soon followed his order, they had felt his full wrath and knew he was not playing. Not saying a word he continued to stare at everyone who was still standing, one at a time. He was daring them to defy him, to go against his will. Anyone who dared challenge him, he stared straight into their eyes, deep into their souls, cuckolding their confidence. After no more than a minute or two everyone was sat down in silence.

"That's good, that's very good everyone. Now put on your seat belts please. "When the alarm finishes I will continue," Piere's voice was calm and soothing. It had returned to its' normal peaceful resonance that they had all first encountered when they got on the coach.

It took another few minutes but eventually the alarm stopped. Piere reached into the cab area and pressed another button. Unbeknownst to the passengers this locked them in place. It was for his safety and theirs. He also turned on all the coaches' internal lights so they could all see him clearly and so he could see all of them.

Piere breathed deeply through his nose. Composing himself, making sure that he was calm and collected. It was important at this moment to both reassure himself and his passengers. He looked up and out at them all, singling no one out in particular. He did note Walter was still blissfully staring out of the window without a care in the world but Piere figured he was no threat and that he should proceed as normal.

"Some of you may have worked a few things out, a few of you might be close to working it out but I will clarify everything for," Piere paused not for dramatic effect but to further compose himself, this bit always made him very nervous, "I am Death. I am the Pale Rider. I told you all as much as you entered onto the coach. As I promised you as you all embarked, you are all safe with me. I will keep that promise to you no matter what. The hard part for you is done. You have died. You are no longer Mortal beings and this, this is the last Charabanc that any of you will ever ride!"

Some of the passengers just stared at him in disbelief, some were visibly shaken at the gravity of what they had just been told. Some passengers started to sob gently, couples held hands or hugged their children. No one was screaming or shouting. A few were fighting with their seat belt which was a locked restraint. Those fighting the restraints just flailed about, fighting themselves a bit but more so fighting the truth. Piere just stood firm, he held his right hand in the air for what seemed like 10 minutes but was, in all likelihood, at most a minute until eventually calm descended.

"Calm yourselves, have some decorum. Just breath ladies and gentlemen. Have I any reason to lie to you? Are you in pain or are you suffering?"

Piere paused knowing how important acceptance was. The realisation had dropped and now they needed to accept. They all needed to accept they had died.

"You are currently thinking I am some prophet of doom; I am not. I am your guide; I am your helper. I am the one soul helping you at this moment. My sole purpose is to escort you on this journey. Some of you are still fighting it, stop fighting it. Fighting is for the living."

Piere looked at the coachful of passengers. Making sure he made eye contact with as many as possible. Making sure he stared hard at them. The sooner they were calm then the sooner the journey could continue. He noted that Walter still hadn't reacted. Perhaps he was the calmest man he ever met, that or he was the first dead person to ever suffer with a full on heart attack.

"It's not as hard as you think. You all told me as you got on how you had died. You all knew then, I have not told you a thing you did not already know. Your minds at the moment might be glossing over it. But you know. You know you are dead; all you have to do is accept the facts."

Piere watched their reactions. Some people were clearly thinking deeply. Some were trying to remember. The problem with memory is humans often tried to blank out anything horrific. It was a natural survival instinct. Piere knew himself, he'd been there, he'd been in their shoes. Many eons ago, he too had fought the truth, he'd fought it hard but eventually had accepted that the life he knew was over, however, in some format, life goes on.

"Ok folks, ok. I'll prove it to you. D3 and D4 the Pearce's. Lovely lads, love their mother and father. However they think it's ok to ride a tandem bicycle at high speed down a mountain side into a parked car without wearing helmets. It's simple physics. You died. A3 and A4 the Thomas's think it's ok to go to an anniversary meal and then go drink driving. Have you guys not seen the adverts telling you not to do that?"

The brothers and the Thomas's all looked at him in complete shock.

"But you knew you were dead. Nothing else could've made sense."

As Piere stood there looking at everyone, Rachel Freeman raised her hand.

"Rachel this isn't school ask away freely, what would you like to share with everyone?"

"I think I did know. I'm sure I did but I was so happy not to be in hospital that I didn't mind. I was worried it was a dream and that I would wake up and I would be hooked up to those horrific machines again."

"Rachel, that's very honest of you. I can promise you that there are no more machines. That is over, it's done. The next stage of your journey is about to begin, in fact with this trip it has begun."

As Piere stood and looked at the aisle. The atmosphere was becoming much calmer. He noted Samuel Ellis with his arm in the air.

"Samuel?"

"And us? How did we get here? What are we doing here?"

"Samuel it's tough. War is brutal. You know where you were. You know what you were doing. Is it really that big of a surprise to you? Do you think 8 soldiers just got transferred together? Of course you don't. That's the rules of engagement, you knew that when you signed up."

"And us? We watched our house burn!"

"No you saw the aftermath and then you met my colleagues who told you where to go. You fried in that fire, and you know it. Do you remember escaping? No of course you don't because you didn't."

"Ok Mr. Darl how do you explain me? Why am I here?"

"Leanne you were 94 years old. You just ran out of life, you just expired darling."

"But I had so much to give and teach."

"And Leanne many on here had much to learn, I don't the make rules I just make sure that they are adhered to."

At that point the first field dweller, Michael Newman, stood up. Piere could see he was really wrestling with his emotions. He didn't actually say anything, he was too overwrought to be able formulate a sentence.

"Michael I am afraid that you and Tyronne were overwhelmed by the weather. It peaked at minus 1 degrees centigrade. You know how Hypothermia works. But you too felt no pain, it just happened. It's tragic for your family and friends, but for you it's just a stepping stone on the road."

Michael knew full well what Piere had told him, he understood the gravity of it without a shadow of a doubt. He had even helped in mountain rescues himself and he just sat back down and patted his friend Tyronne on the leg. It was fuzzy in his mind but he thought he could remember the clouds closing in, the temperature dropping and the two of them huddling together in a crevice for warmth. It made sense to him. He knew the odds but it still shook him to his core.

Piere was looking everywhere trying to make sure that they all understood the situation, that this was the inevitable consequence of life. They were getting it. It was sinking in. It was taking time but Piere felt that they were now all roughly on the same hymn sheet.

"And me? What did I do? What did David do?"

Piere looked at Mrs. Mumford cradling the 6 months old David. He was awake now and giggling away as babies do when they're not crying or pooping. He placed his hand on her shoulder trying to make her know that she had his full attention.

"Mrs. Mumford. David did nothing, nothing at all, he just existed, however briefly, and you did your best with no support. You fought the good fight but some days you can fight no longer. And I'm assuming that you decided David was better off with you rather than there without you."

"Are you saying I killed David?"

"I'm saying you know the truth. I'm saying you fought as hard as you could for as long as you could. You know exactly what I'm saying. You did all you could and then you made choices for him."

"Will he always be six months old?"

"I don't make those decisions. That's not my department. I transport people."

"When will I know? When will he know?"

"Soon enough."

The whole coach was now in silence, the conversation about David had sapped the energy out of most. Accidents happen but this was a completely different can of worms. Piere breathed easy for the first time in what felt like a long time. He let everyone just take a moment to accept where they were at.

"Right folks, it's simple now. I cannot guide you anymore. I can assist, I can listen but the truth is something that you all must take on board. You must all accept your own truths. The memories will come back. Embrace them, they are, after all, yours.

Right we are parked in a layby. I, myself am gonna go have a cigarette. I will unlock your seat belts, if you want to step out for some air and a walk around, then that is cool. But in 10 minutes the coach will be departing and if you want the answers you crave you will be on it."

Piere leant into the cab and unlocked the seat belts and then he undid the coach door. Finally he strolled down the few steps and out into the very cold early morning air. He went and lent against the front of the coach and waited to see what would happen. He had done all he could. These situations often worked themselves out. He was pleased he had got as close to the destination as he did before everything unraveled.

The first person down the steps to him was Michelle Ovette. She had taken her stilettos off and turned to face him as she hit the ground.

"You got a light sweetie?"

Piere obliged and lit her cigarette.

"I suppose I was always a candidate for this sort of thing, wasn't I?"

"Michelle we are all guaranteed candidates it's just more a question of when your time is up. The body, the physical body can only take so much and being fair from what your report tells me, you had your monies worth out of that vessel."

Michelle smiled and at the same time looked a little sad. Perhaps regretful of how it has all played out.

"I'd have liked longer."

"But would you change anything?"

"Hell no, I had a blast."

"Then I guess you've answered your own question about regret."

"So how long am I gonna be like this."

"Well Michelle I can not tell you that, all I can say is enjoy the journey."

Michelle laughed heartily and reached into her bag. She produced a hip flask of alcohol. Looked straight at Piere and before he could say a word she unscrewed the lid and swallowed the entire contents.

"Now Piere before you say a thing sweetie, you said no alcohol on the coach and I am very clearly not on the coach."

"You are correct and I cannot argue one iota. Michelle you should've been a lawyer."

"Piere I could have been many things."

Piere smiled and noticed that most people were now outside the coach. He also saw that the man mountain Mr. Potter was making his towards him at a rate of knots..

"Mr. Potter how can I help?"

Mr. Potter stopped short of Piere by maybe 4 inches. Looking straight down at him he asked.

"It was the cooker wasn't it?"

"No Mr. Potter."

Mr. Potter stared even more intently at Piere than he had 3 seconds previously.

"If it wasn't the cooker what was it?"

"It was the gas that didn't get to the cooker. It was just a good thing you lived in a detached house."

"I bloody knew it. I'm such a prick."

"Mr. Potter look at it from a different perspective. You're all together. You have your family with you. You always will have and age is now irrelevant."

"Did we suffer?"

"Do you remember suffering?"

Mr. Potter stood expressionless looking at Piere.

"No, I don't remember a thing really."

Piere looked at Mr. Potter and smiled.

"That answers your question then. It's the same as do you remember being born?"

Mr. Potter patted him on the shoulder, nearly breaking it. *Bloody giants* thought Piere. Mr. Potter knew that that ended their conversation as much as Piere hoped it was.

Piere watched as his passengers talked about their shared experiences. He stabbed his cigarette out and decided that their break had been quite long enough. He was just about to round everyone up when the eldest of James' brother approached. He looked tearful and was very clearly having trouble summoning up the courage to face Piere.

"Did I kill him? Is it my fault my little brother is dead?"

"James you are asking several question. Are you ultimately responsible? I wouldn't say you were. Yes you invited Jarrod to the gig, you took him along, you were trying to show your brother a good time. Perhaps trying to be the cool older brother. Are you actually responsible? Course not. You thought you were going to a cool underground gig. Is it your fault that the security was lapse? No. Is it your fault they got greedy and let to many in? No, of course not. I will give you a piece of advice though. When you're dead carrying guilt is not gonna help you. You gotta let it go. I know it's hard to see but you thought that your night out would be cool and it would have been if others had been as cool as you. Let it go. It's now pointless."

Piere watched as James wiped his eyes on his sleeve. He was upset, he was emotional but Piere hoped that soon enough he would see being dead wasn't the end of the world. It was, after all, the inevitable consequence of life.

Piere looked at Mrs. Kennedy who was looking at him in with a very confused expression. Her eyes fixated on him.

"Is this a bad dream Piere? Is this a nightmare I shall wake from?" she asked solemnly.

"No Mrs. Kennedy. This is your new reality."

"But I haven't felt this well in ages, in a long time. I can breathe, I can walk without getting breathless," she exclaimed.

"Of course you can. Your mortal fatigues are gone. They are no longer a constraint," Piere said trying to explain the shift in realities to her.

"But how? I was feeling better, I was feeling much better!"

"I think Phillip knows," Piere said.

"Phillip knows? How would Phillip know? He was fit as a fiddle, why is he here? Explain that!" Mrs. Kennedy was getting angry. She was at a stage of grief where she was grasping at straws and bemoaning the loss of her previous existence.

"Mrs. Kennedy. I believe Phillip took his vows of 'in sickness and in health forever and ever' very seriously and thus he would never leave your side and nor could he see you suffer any further," Piere bowed his head and prayed Phillip would say something, anything.

"Darling, it's a bit fuzzy and I don't really remember much between the hotel room and the bus stop but I think we....I am pretty sure we decided enough was enough, that we had had a wonderful time and that we could chose our own endings," Phillip said with tears forming in his eyes.

"Oh Phillip you could've lived for many years without me," Mrs. Kennedy said.

"No Diane, I could've existed for a few more years but without you I wouldn't haven't been living."

The two of them embraced like the teenagers they once were and Piere left them to have their moment. Sometimes people's love for one another was so strong it could even affect him.

After a few more minutes watching everyone begin to accept their choices and fates that enough was enough, they had eternity to work this all out.

Piere watched as Jarrod put his arm around James, that together those two would be alright. He watched many embracing, the Kennedy's were still smooching like teenagers and thus he breathed in deeply, making sure he had a lung full and called out to everyone outside the coach,

"Ladies and gentlemen please get back on the coach. I am paid by the mile not the number of passengers. Thus if I lose you, I lose you, and I still get paid!"

As was normal everyone did as they were told. The futility of warring against the grain was over. They were all now slightly intrigued as to what was next.

Piere watched and waited until Walter went to board the coach. Piere tried hard to act as cool as possible but Walter had got under his skin. He barred Walter's access as everyone else got on board. Once satisfied that they were alone, with no one listening in, he offered Walter a cigarette which was declined. Piere lit his cigarette and squared himself to look at Walter.

"You knew! You knew the whole time and not only did you not say a word you didn't mind. How? Why?"

Piere was quite animated as he tried to find out the truth from Walter.

"Son it's easy. I've had a pacemaker for over twenty years. When I got on this coach I couldn't feel it nor could I hear it. I knew my heart wouldn't work without it so there were only two options. Either I had somehow developed an immunity to reality or I was dead. And being dead was the more likely and then as people got on it just made more sense that we were all dead. It wasn't a hard transition to make. I tested it by holding my breath and after 15 minutes, when I didn't pass out, I had confirmed my hypothesis."

Piere laughed and shook his head.

"I like you Walter. We're gonna get on just fine. Now let's get these other buggers back on the coach," Piere laughed heartily. He liked characters like Walter they made his life easy for both himself and for themselves, they just sort of go with the flow.

"COME ON BACK ON THE COACH EVERYONE PLEASE!!"

As soon as they were all on Piere embarked himself. He shut the door and stood at the end of the aisle as they all got themselves settled. Once sure that they were all happy and secure Piere began to talk to them.

"Ladies and Gentlemen I have done this trip over a thousand times; I've told innumerate people this simple piece of advice and I hope it resonates with you as well. 13.8 billion year ago there was a big bang and you were created, every particle that exists in you is that old. You have existed here on Earth as a sentient being, all of you, for less than 100 years. This means that for roughly the same 13.8 billion years you didn't exist and it didn't hurt, it caused you no harm whatsoever. So you have nothing to fear. Therefore just enjoy the ride, your last ever ride on my Charabanc!"

With that Piere sat back in the drivers' seat of the coach. He didn't turn the seat belt warning light on, he didn't dim the aisle lights he just let it ride. He checked the mirrors and pulled out onto the main road, accelerating smoothly away from the layby. They didn't know it yet but this was just the start of their journey. Piere smiled, relaxing fully into the heated drivers' seat, he wondered if he really could get his heated seat upgraded to a heated massaging driver's seat for his next trip, food for thought on another day he decided and he made his mind up to just enjoy the rest of his journey and the start of theirs!!

ABOUT THE AUTHOR

J. C. Jones is regarded by many who know him as a legend in his lunchbreak. A man who gets hungry whilst eating and tired whilst sleeping. He is man of few words which makes being an author very difficult.

Printed in Great Britain
by Amazon